The Deacon Of Dobbinsville
A Story Based On Actual Happenings

By

John A. Morrison

The Deacon Of Dobbinsville
A Story Based On Actual Happenings
by John A. Morrison

ISBN: 978-93-61159-02-2
Published by

DOUBLE 9 BOOKS

2/13-B, Ansari Road
Daryaganj, New Delhi – 110002
info@double9books.com
www.double9books.com
Tel. 011-40042856

ABOUT THE AUTHOR

John A. Morrison, the author of "The Deacon of Dobbinsville," is a literary craftsman whose storytelling prowess brings to lifestyles the quaint and interesting international of Dobbinsville. Morrison paintings displays a deep understanding of human nature, community dynamics, and the undying subject matters that resonate with readers throughout generations. In "The Deacon of Dobbinsville," Morrison showcases his potential to create richly textured characters and immersive settings. The narrative unfolds in Dobbinsville, a place that will become a canvas for exploring the complexities of small-city life, relationships, and the intricacies of human interactions. Morrison's keen observations and nuanced portrayals breathe lifestyles into the characters, making them relatable and remarkable. The identify, "The Deacon of Dobbinsville," recommendations at an important person who likely performs a pivotal function inside the story. Deacons regularly symbolize pillars of the community, individuals with ethical authority and a dedication to service. Morrison, along with his literary finesse, may additionally delve into the demanding situations, triumphs, and personal increase of the deacon man or woman, presenting readers with a narrative that goes beyond the floor.

CONTENTS

CHAPTER I

Mount Olivet church at the time of which I am about to write had received the zenith of her glory. She was possessed of a full measure of the denominational pride and prejudice common to the day and the community in which she existed. Since Mount Olivet church is to occupy so conspicuous a place in my narrative, it is fitting that I should take time and space right here to describe her. I must also give my readers an idea of the community of which Mount Olivet church formed the hub and center.

Well, to begin with, Mount Olivet church was old. And like, all other things old she had a history, partly respectable and partly otherwise. The date of her organization reached back into the fifties, before the days of the Civil War. Some great notables had lived and died in this church. Tradition had it that one of the charter members of this church was a candidate for president of the United States against James Buchanan. Of course he was not elected, as you know, and I suppose you have noticed nothing in our national history about this particular man running for president, but you recall that the history of a nation and the history of a local country district have a way of reading differently.

But this aspirant to the presidential office was not the only great man who had been a member of Mount Olivet church. The older citizens told of a certain Preacher Crookshank who was pastor of this church during and prior to the Civil War and was also a member of the State Legislature; and, according to these biographers, he was the sole cause of the State remaining in the Union. It seems from all reports that Preacher Crookshank was not only a statesman of renown, but also a masterful theologian of Mount Olivet's particular faith. It is reported how he defended his theology with his splendid oratory, and how when this failed he resorted to his fists. His oratory was said to be simply overwhelming. They recounted how, in his oratorical frenzies, he used to fling his homespun coat in the air and crack the heels of his red-topped boots together with an emphasis that would stop the mouth of the most impudent gainsayer. They told how by this masterful eloquence opposers were silenced, heretics were brought to orthodoxy, and infidels were converted. Preacher Crookshank flourished contemporaneously with John Barleycorn. To be frank, he and John were bosom friends. In fact, it was reported that Crookshank was never at his best in preaching except when he had an infilling of the "spirit" of the Barleycorn type. He had a certain long-tailed coat, said to have been given to him by a fellow member of the Legislature. This coat had large pockets in the tail wherein was carried a bottle of whiskey. This was a source of much inspiration to Crookshank throughout his long and eventful career.

But I must leave off any further description of this notable. Those who are further interested I refer to the blue-grass cemetery just back of Mount Olivet church, where a tombstone is to be found bearing this inscription: "Rev. John Crookshank--Statesman, Preacher, Orator. Died June 6, 1867."

As before stated, Mount Olivet church flourished. She was nestled among the picturesque Ozark Hills, about midway between Ridgetown and Dobbinsville. Everybody in the community, almost, who had any religious inclination, and some who had none, belonged to Mount Olivet. She boasted in being the largest church in all Randolph County--the churches at Ridgetown and Dobbinsville not excepted. When I say that Mount Olivet church flourished, I do not mean that she flourished in spiritual things. Indeed, her candle of vital religion had well-nigh flickered out. Scarcely a member could be found who would testify to a real experience of salvation from sin. There were three things for which the members of this particular church were remarkable, namely, they were great sticklers for the faith of their church, they were all holiness-fighters, they all used tobacco in some form.

CHAPTER II

Deacon Gramps sat on his plow-handles. The sultry August day was drawing to a close. The sun was just ready to roll its bright red disk behind the western horizon. The Deacon seemed to be in a deep meditation. He cast a glance at his beautiful farm as it stretched itself out for a mile toward the river on the one side and nestled snugly against the foot of the limestone hill on the other side. The large white farmhouse with green trimming cozily planted on a blue-grass knoll across the brook seemed to bid him be at rest. The large red barn just back of the house stood out in sharp contrast against the green-foliaged mountain. The gold-colored balls on the lightning rods glistened in the farewell rays of the receding sun. Mount Olivet Church reared her white walls modestly from the brow of the blue-grass knoll a quarter of a mile eastward. Deacon Gramps was, at the close of this peaceful summer day, indulging in a mental congratulation of himself on being so favorably situated in life. Everybody recognized Farmer Gramps as being the wealthiest man in all Spruce Township. He owned the finest and fattest horses that were driven to Mount Olivet Church. His cattle roamed the forests for miles around, and his hogs cracked acorns on every hillside.

Apart from his worldly wealth he was the most distinguished member of Mount Olivet church. For years he had been deacon in said church, and was president of the official board. In fact, he was as truly a part of the Church as was the pulpit on the platform or the bell in the steeple. No meeting was complete without him. He was an indispensable part of the service. He always sat in the same pew, and none coming into the Church previously to Deacon Gramps ever dared sit in his pew any more than they dared to monopolize the preacher's chair in the pulpit. He always enjoyed the double pleasure of chewing his tobacco and hearing the sermon simultaneously, and this necessitated his occupying a pew near the window, as you may well suppose. This window was known to roguish boys as "Deacon Window" and not even the bravest of these boys dared peep through this window during services as was their custom in the case of the other windows.

Perhaps it is needless to say that the uninterrupted presence of Gramps had a profound influence upon the service. No preacher dared to fail to recognize his dignity. As well as being an officer in the church he was the heaviest contributor to its collections. He had a very curious habit of twitching his right ear when the preacher said something that did not just set well with him, and it naturally followed that every pastor who ever served Mount Olivet fell into the habit of watching Gramp's ear, and of course the sermon was governed accordingly. Thus "According to the deacon's ear," came to be a by-word through the community.

Well, as I have already said, Deacon Gramps sat on his plow-handles. Just as he turned to unfasten the trace-chains from the plow to drive his horses to the barn, he saw two men climbing over the whitewashed fence that led from the barn toward the Church on the hill. Seeing these men were coming towards him, he resumed his position on the plow-handles and waited for them. As the two men drew near, he recognized in them the familiar features of Deacon Brown and Deacon Jones.

CHAPTER III

Jake Benton was a member of Mount Olivet Church and had been for twenty-seven years. Jake was a man of ordinary natural intelligence, but like most of his neighbors was utterly ignorant as far as literary training is concerned. He naturally had deep religious sentiments. Under proper teaching he doubtless would have pressed his way into a genuine experience of salvation and would have lived a consistent Christian life, but under the unwholesome teachings of Mount Olivet he had given himself over to a mighty religious drift and had drifted far away from God and was completely destitute of redeeming grace. Oh, to be sure, he testified regularly at the church services and gave of his limited means toward the church's support, but he was a man of uncontrollable temper and was well versed in the art of old-fashioned fist-fighting. But his profession had become a burden to him, and he had often wondered if there were no possibility of extracting some joy out of the juiceless lemon of his profession.

Now, it so happened one summer that Deacon Cramps had a large drove of cattle ranging on the hills about thirty miles to the southeast of Mount Olivet community. This drove of cattle consisted of a thousand head, and it became necessary that the Deacon employ some trustworthy person to herd the cattle and prevent them from scattering, or being stolen by cattle-thieves who sometimes visited that section. Since Jake Benton was known as an upright man and was a brother in the church, Deacon Cramps offered him the position. Out of pure financial necessity Jake accepted.

This was some years before the rubber-tired automobile had invaded the flint hills of this section and thirty miles meant hours of toilsome travel. Thus it was necessary that Jake take along a camping outfit and remain all summer. This he decided to do. Many and long were the hours that Jake spent in this lonely mountain retreat. For miles around there was little sign of human activity. No sound of woodman's ax was heard. The stillness of the long summer afternoons was broken only by the tinkling of the bells on the hillsides. A lone log cabin lifted its mud-chinked walls from the brow of a hill from under which flowed a babbling stream of clear water. In the attic of this lone cabin Jake Benton was regularly lulled to sleep by the evening lullabies of the katydids as they sang in the tops of the postoak trees with which the cabin was surrounded.

One August afternoon when Jake returned from his regular roundup of the cattle, he found, seated on a log near the spring, two men. At the sight of the men Jake's heart leaped into his mouth. For two months he had not laid his eyes on a human form. He had heard no human voice save his own. Needless to say, he was as much pleased as surprised to find companions in his lonely abode. Jake neared the log where the men sat. One of them arose and advanced toward him. "I trust," he remarked, "that you will not think we are trespassing on your premises. We have been traveling all day; our horses were tired and we were thirsty, and the spring invited us to be refreshed." For a moment Jake stood speechless, and then in almost forgotten terms he made his unexpected visitors feel welcome.

The three men conversed for some time, and in the course of the conversation Jake explained to them the reason for his lonely life and the circumstances that caused him to be thus engaged. The strangers explained that they were driving across the State, and that, in order to make their journey fifty miles shorter, they had been instructed to take this untraveled road through this expanse of wooded hills.

"I should think," remarked one of the men, "that this would be a splendid place to meditate on the goodness of God. Loneliness often begets meditation, and God loves to be the companion of the companionless. Then, too, there is all this nature with which you are surrounded. These flowers and trees and birds all speak of the goodness of God. I was remarking to my fellow traveler of how these beautiful scenes remind us of God's goodness. Pardon a frank question, but may I ask, Are you saved?"

This was all new language to Jake and he scarcely knew how to answer this rather blunt question. "Wu-wu-well, ye-yes," he answered. "I try to be a Christian. I belong to the church and have belonged for twenty-seven years and accordin' to the preachin' we have I think I'll get to heaven. I s'pose you fellers must be preachers."

"Yes, we are preachers," remarked the other. "We have consecrated our lives to the blessed service of Christ and our greatest delight is in preaching his gospel and telling others of the wonders of his grace. There can be no higher calling than that of telling of the saving grace of God. For fifteen years I was a cold professor of religion, but I lacked vital salvation. I belonged to the church and paid the preacher, and somehow I thought I would get through all right. I sinned more or less every day and did not know that I could be saved from sin. In fact, I never had been converted. I tried to live a Christian life, but I was powerless. After fifteen years of this miserable existence I got a new vision of things. God removed the scales from my eyes and I saw my lost condition. I saw myself in an entirely new light. I wept before God because of my sins. I was made very conscious that unless I was saved from my sins they would damn me in hell forever. My churchianity and my self-righteousness and my morality looked ridiculous when I saw myself a sinner in the sight of God. I came to God and poured out my soul in bitter repentance, and said, 'Save me, or I perish.' I promised him that I would forsake my sins, make my wrongs right, and walk in the light. I read in 1 John 1:9, 'If we confess our sins, he is faithful and just to forgive us our sins, and to cleanse us from all unrighteousness.' Well, I confessed my sins and forsook them, and God for Christ's sake pardoned all my sins. Praise His name. The joy and peace that filled my soul were unspeakable. I was a new man. I loved everybody, even my bitter enemies. Christ, in all his blessed reality, came into my heart as an abiding companion. Some time after my conversion, through a holiness paper, which fell into my hands, and through reading the Bible, which had become a new book to me, I learned that it was possible for me to be wholly sanctified and to have the Holy Spirit as an abiding comforter. Oh, the joy of this blessed life. Its glories are untold."

Poor Jake stood amazed. He had never heard anything like this before. He burst out, "If that's religion, I confess I hain't got none; and to be plain, I ain't much inclined to believe such stuff as that. I have been a member of Mount Olivet Church for twenty-seven years and I never heard such preaching as that. That must be some new religion that's goin' around. Talk about bein' saved from sin, why there's our dear old Brother Simms, who was our last pastor at Mount Olivet. He died last March and since then we ain't had no pastor--why I heard him say more'n once from the pulpit that folks can't be saved from sin till they get to heaven."

All this Jake said and a great deal more. He talked himself hoarse and used up all his choicest terms in extolling the name of Mount Olivet Church and all the pastors she had had since he had been a member. All his arguments were quietly and lovingly answered by the ministers, who read to him many passages of Scripture.

By this time the large elm cast a lengthy shadow eastward. The sun was well-nigh set, and it was evident to the ministers that they should have to prevail on their new acquaintance to lodge them overnight.

"Well, my dear brother," remarked one of the ministers, "we are far apart in faith, but I trust we are all honest in our views and I pray that God may lead us all in the way we should go. The day is gone, and to get out of these hills tonight is unthinkable. I wonder if you could arrange to keep us overnight, Mr. Benton--I believe that's the name? If you will, we shall be a hundred times obliged and shall be glad to pay you whatever you suggest."

Jake was big hearted, if he was a sinner. "Sure, I'll keep ye, think I'd turn anybody out in these woods at night? Not me. I've kept preachers all my life, but I confess I never kept sanctified ones before."

The three men went up the hill to Jake's cabin, and the two ministers busied themselves writing letters while Jake prepared the evening meal from his scant pantry. When they had gathered around the large goods-box that served as a dining-table, one of the preachers thanked God for the food and asked his blessings upon it. When the evening meal was finished, the three men sat in front of Jake's cabin until a late hour. The preachers expounded the Scriptures to poor, ignorant Jake and told him of the wonders of God's grace. Finally, when the big silvery moon stood in mid-heaven and the sound of cow-bells on the hill had died away, Jake suggested that they retire for the night. By the light of the moon one of the ministers read his Bible. It so happened that he opened it at the 12th chapter of Hebrews. These words as they fell from this man's pious lips affected Jake deeply. He surely had read that same chapter himself many times, and doubtless during the twenty-seven years he had been a member of Mount Olivet Church he had heard his pastor read it. But there was one verse that sank right to the center of Jake's heart. It was the 14th: "Follow peace with all men, and holiness, without which no man shall see the Lord." Jake had always had a hope in his breast that he should some day see the Lord. He had had more than his allotted share of troubles in life, and deep in his heart he had a longing to go where "the wicked cease from troubling and the weary be at rest."

Soon all was silence in the cabin attic, where the three men lay. The restless surgings of man's inner soul are invisible to all eyes, save God's, and silence is not always a proof that everyone is asleep. Jake lay on a bag of dried leaves, having given his own bunk to his guests. But his eyes refused to sleep. The music of the katydids had lost its power to soothe his troubled breast and bring him sweet repose. His mind took a voyage over the past. Memory, according to her wonted ways carried him again to his mother's knee. He recalled the sound of her voice as she sang, "When I shall see Him face to face and tell the story saved by grace." But that scripture, "Without holiness no man shall see the Lord," took the sweetness out of that long-remembered song. Jake knew he was not holy. His heart was defiled by sin. His lips were unclean with blaspheming God's name. He remembered all the good resolutions he had made and broken the past quarter of a century. And during these midnight musings he seemed to see two lily-white hands beckoning him to come somewhere; he knew not where. These hands he readily recognized as the hands of his own baby Rose, who had gone from him one day near the close of her fifth summer. Mentally he found himself again at the bedside of his darling Rose. He saw again her ruddy cheeks glow with fever and heard the tremble of her voice as she said, "Daddy's

Rose is going to heaven. Daddy come some day." Again he saw the death-glare in the sky-blue eyes when the little soul flitted away. He saw himself again as he sat and looked into the sweet and lifeless face of his darling girl, and he remembered how he resolved on that day to live in such a way as to be reunited with his child. But his resolves had all been unfilled, and he saw the path of his past strewn with broken vows. In reality, God was speaking to the man's soul. Jake saw himself in his true condition, a lost sinner. His sins seemed like horrid black mountains rearing themselves eternally between him and his child. His profession of religion and his church-membership seemed to mock him rather than to comfort him.

But Jake was silent. He said not a word with his lips; but how his bleeding heart did talk to God. Hot tears flowed from his sleepless eyes and dampened the dry leaves that formed his pillow. He supposed the two ministers asleep. Their opinion of him was the same. Finally Jake was astonished to see, in the glimmering light of the moon that stole through the cracks in the clapboard roof, the two preachers slip from their bed, and kneel on the floor. His ear caught their whispering prayers that were heard in heaven. As nearly as he could hear, the prayers ran something like this: "O Lord, thou didst have a purpose in sending us through these wooded hills. May we be instrumental in bringing light and salvation to this lonely cabin. Lord, talk to the heart of this Mr. Benton, who sleeps on his bag of leaves. Bring something before his mind that will break up his heart; disturb him even in his sleep, Lord."

Jake's emotions overwhelmed him and he could keep silent no longer. He bounded from his bed, crying, "O my God, save me, save me, save me! Oh, do pray for me now! I am lost! lost! lost!"

Needless to say, the preachers were somewhat shocked, as people often are when their prayers are answered sooner than they expect. The convicted herdsman prostrated himself on the floor before the preachers and poured out bitter tears of repentance. He wept and groaned, and begged God to save him. But he seemed slow to grasp God's promises. He prayed till the morning dawned. The preachers prayed with him. Finally, just as the first grey streaks of the new day began to creep between the logs, Jake's faith was anchored in God's promises, and the glory of heaven flooded his soul. In the twinkling of an eye he was made a new man. His joy knew no bounds. He leaped and shouted, sang and whistled, and laughed and cried, all for the joy of his new-found treasure.

When breakfast was over and the two ministers had bidden their new convert a happy farewell, Jake sat down to read his Bible, which the preachers had given him. His eyes fell upon these words, "Weeping may endure for a night, but joy cometh in the morning." (Psa. 30:5).

CHAPTER IV

The anteroom of the post office in a little Ohio town was crowded. The train had arrived from the west, but it went as soon as it came, for it did not stop. A scream of the whistle, the rumble of the wheels, and the mighty monster dashed through the peaceful town at fifty miles an hour. But the inhabitants were not so interested in the train, for they had seen it pass in just this fashion year after year. But from the baggage coach there came each evening a bag of mail, and this was the cause of the gathering at the post office. While the postmaster and his assistant were opening and distributing the mail behind the closed window in the post office, the restless townspeople occupied themselves in social chat discussing the local happenings of the day, or in reading the notices on the bulletin board.

Everybody was at the post office at this hour. School children, happy at the close of an irksome day of school, shouted boisterously at each other in the street. Laboring men, with empty dinner pails in hand, sat restfully on the curbstone just outside the post office door, and talked of the happenings of the day. The village blacksmith wiped the honest sweat from his brow, closed the shop door, and came down to the post office, where he was met by his flaxen-haired girl of three summers. She clasped her pink arms about the smith's grimy neck and told him Mama was looking for a letter from Grandma, who had gone to California for her health, and that she had come down to see how many kisses Grandma had sent her. The town doctor, with a dignified air, leaned against the side of the post office door and read the Chicago paper that a previous mail had brought to him. The schoolmaster had finished grading some test papers and had come down to the post office just in time to be the third party to an interesting fist fight in which two sixth grade boys were engaged with great zest, in the street. Two out-of-town strangers, who were guests at the hotel just across the way, came over and, seating themselves on a bench in front of the post office engaged in conversation.

Finally the task behind the window was done. The mail was sorted and placed alphabetically in the proper boxes. The postmaster flipped up the window, and there was a mighty rush and a scramble--for who is not eager to get a letter? Some received several letters and papers; some only one letter; some only a paper; some only a catalogue. Some were disappointed altogether, judging from facial expressions; some received glad messages, some sad messages, some indifferent.

When the crowd was dispersed, the two strangers who had been seated on the bench appeared at the window and called for their mail. The postmaster handed to one of them a letter addressed, Evangelist Blank. The address was written in almost an unreadable hand. The evangelist opened the letter. It ran thus:

Dobbinsville, ----, Aug. 29----

My dear Evangelist brother:

i am saved and sanctified praise God O how i rejoice in this wonderful salvashun i was a member of Mt. Olivet church fer 27 yrs. but i never knowed what it was to be saved from sin this summer i was herdin cattle down in the hills about 30 mi. from here and a most wonderful thing happened. To preachers came along and told me that Christ could save and sanctify me i fought them at first but God would not let me rest until i gave him my heart, then he sanctified me holy o how i rejoice my wife and oldest son is also saved now but say bruther how the people of my own church persecute me they say I am crazy and that a man cant be saved from sin in this life o if i had only found this salvashun when i was a young man but now i am middle aged but by god's grace i aim to do all i can to save my neighbors, i see in the holiness paper that you are a evangelist and that you go about preachin this wonderful salvashun so i want to now if you will come down here and preach to the people we can't get Mt. Olivet church but we can build a brush arber. i am sending you $20. this part of the money i urned herdin cattle for deacon gramps i promised the Lord when he saved me that i would give him part of this money so here it is so i hope you can cum your brother saved sanctified and happy

Jake Benton

CHAPTER V

As I have said before, Deacon Gramps sat on his plow handles at the close of an August day. He fairly rejoiced when he saw Deacon Brown and Deacon Jones coming toward him.

"Good evening, Brother Gramps," shouted Jones and Brown simultaneously.

"Good evening, my good brethering," responded Gramps, "I am so glad to see you. I have a great burden on my mind and I was just planning to go to your house, Brother Brown, as soon as I had unharnessed my team and eaten supper."

Brown and Jones looked at Gramps with an expectant gaze, and continued silent. Gramps went on, "It's high time we was doin' somethin' to protect our church. I have been a deacon in this church fer many a year, but to my mind this is the most dangerous time Mount Olivet has ever seen."

Brown and Jones nodded a candid assent to what was being said. Gramps continued, "For many years our church has been the strongest church in this county and everybody has counted it an honor to belong to this church, but you know, brethering, ever since our pastor died last spring, and we have been without a pastor we have been gettin' weaker and weaker. And since old Jake Benton has gone crazy over this new religion of hisen he is trien to get everybody else to go crazy. You brethering knows how I sent him down in the hills this summer to mind cattle. Well he seemed to kinder git overbalanced in his mind down there and he's found a new religion. You know how he testified in meetin' tother night. He said he was saved from sin and he said he was sanctified, and whole lot of other stuff like that. And I believe he said, didn't he, that he was just as good as Jesus Christ and gettin' better ever' day, or something like that."

"Yes, something like that," added Brown.

"Yes," said Jones, "I was there myself and heard him. I have always thought Jake Benton was a pretty good man; but when a feller gets so good as all that, then he's too good for this world. You know the Bible says there's nobody good but God."

"Yes, I've heard the best preachers that was ever pastor of Mount Olivet Church and they all say we sin a thousand times every day," remarked Gramps.

Jones spoke next: "I knew a bunch of them holiness people back in South Caroliner where I come from. They was the most outrageous bunch of people I ever saw. Why, they claimed that they couldn't sin, and that they was just as good as Jesus Christ and that nobody would get to heaven but them. I'll tell you brethering we must not let them get the start here. If they do, Mount Olivet Church is ruined. They tear down churches just as fast as they come to 'em. Old Jake Benton ought to be run out of the country or else sent to the asylum. He ain't fit to run at large. Why, he told Aunt Sally Perkins that he was wholly sanctified and that his heart was just as pure as that of his little baby that died years ago when Jake lived over on Persimmon Ridge. He talks a whole lot now about goin' to meet his baby and his mother and he seems to get so happy every time he talks about it." Jones's voice trembled slightly as he went on to say, "But brethering, it makes me feel most wonderfully queer when I hear Jake talk about meetin' his little girl. He seems to have no doubt at all about meetin' her, and say, you remember my little boy died the same fall as Jake's little girl, and to tell the truth I'm just a little fearful at times about bein' ready to meet little George."

Deacon Gramps listened to all of this from Jones rather restlessly. He spoke next with great gravity. "Brethering, since I am president of this Board of Deacons I feel it my duty to take steps to see that this new religion is stopped and that Mount Olivet Church is not torn to pieces. As I said, I have been deacon here for many years and I have never seen the church so in danger. Something must be done. I'll tell you what we need, we need a preacher--one of our very best ones to come here and fight this devilish holiness stuff."

"That's what we need, we must wipe holiness out," responded Brown, as he let go a sluice of tobacco juice.

Gramps continued, "Just today I had a letter from a cousin of mine back in Kentucky. He says they have a wonderful preacher back there by the name of Preacher Bonds. He says this Preacher Bonds feels a special call to fight holiness. I tell you, brethering, if we could get him here we would make it hot for old Benton and his bunch."

"We would that," Jones chimed in.

"Brother Gramps, why don't you write and ask Preacher Bonds to come?" suggested Brown. "Although the other two members of the Board are not here, I think we just as well go ahead."

"Better bring it before the church," said Gramps, "because we've got to raise some money to get him."

Brown and Jones both agreed that Gramps was right in this respect. With the understanding that Deacon Gramps was to call a meeting of the church at the earliest possible date, the three men separated.

Gramps spent the entire following day riding about the community giving every member of Mount Olivet a personal notification that a special meeting of the church would be held on the following Wednesday evening for the purpose of considering grave problems concerning the church. Wednesday evening came; practically the whole church responded. When the appointed hour arrived, Gramps was on the spot. On every face was written expectancy. Deacon Gramps presided of course. He arose from his seat, flung his quid of tobacco out of the window, squared himself against the pulpit, adjusted his eyeglasses near the point of his nose, and looking over them he addressed the assembly thus: "My brethering and sistern, we have met as members of the grand old Mount Olivet Church. Here in this church our fathers met. Here in this church our mothers met. Here in this church our grandfathers met. Here in this church our grandmothers met. Here in this church, my brethering, we have met. And let me say to you, my dear people, that we have met here tonight in this church for a purpose. There are certain people in this community whose aim is to tear up this church; certain people, I say, whose aim is to tear down this church. There is a certain doctring--the doctring of holiness--getting into this community. This holiness doctring, my friends, is a devilish doctring, my brethering, and must be wiped out." (Amens all over the house.)

All this the Deacon said, and much more. He began his speech with considerable warmth of utterance, but as he progressed in praises of Mount Olivet and her faith he waxed hotter and hotter until his spellbound hearers were fairly deluged in a mighty avalanche of his rustic oratory, and he wound up with the sweeping statement that the doctrine of holiness must be abolished from the face of the earth.

When the Deacon had finished, and regained breath enough to put the matter to a vote, it was unanimously voted that Preacher Bonds should be secured at the earliest date possible.

CHAPTER VI

A year had rolled around since Jake Benton had been converted down in the hills. By this time it was plain to all unbiased minds that Benton was indeed earnest. Even his most bitter enemies were obliged to admit that a mighty change had come over him. His life had undergone a real transformation. His life was an entirely new life. He had unshaken faith in the God of his salvation. In his home he established a family altar, where he worshipped God as regularly as the sun rose and set. In his business relations he literally followed the Golden Rule. At church he unflinchingly declared what his new-found religion had done for him. He declared that God had saved him from his sins and had subsequently sanctified him wholly. He even waxed bold enough to tell in meeting how God had healed him of physical ailments in answer to prayer. All this greatly incensed his fellow church-members. They insisted that he had gone crazy and was no longer fit to belong to the church. Accordingly he was put out. Jake took it all in good part and rejoiced that he was counted worthy to suffer for Jesus' sake.

But Jake was not long obliged to stand alone in defense of his profession. His simple life of trust soon began to have its effect in the community; during the year his faithfulness had been rewarded by the salvation of a number of persons in the neighborhood. Old Grandma Gray had come out boldly on Benton's side. She said that for fifty years she had been living as best she could, but that she had all this time had a longing for the fulness of the blessing, such as Jake Benton testified to, and she arose right in the public meeting and declared herself a seeker for just such a blessing. This set Mount Olivet church all in a storm. Deacon Gramps was furious. He said Jake Benton had a legion of devils and that Grandma Gray was bewitched.

But when Grandma Gray took her stand for full salvation, the cause for which Mount Olivet stood suffered a mighty blow. Nolan Gray, a son with whom Grandma Gray had made her home for years, had been a stanch member of the church since he was a child. In fact, he had always said he had grown up in the church. Nolan Gray was a very upright man of undoubted integrity, and he stood for high moral ideals, but under the type of preaching to which he was accustomed he had never experienced a change of heart. When he saw what a change had come over his mother, he refused to be comforted with his religious profession. Jake Benton was a tenant on Gray's farm, and from daily contact with Benton, Mr. Gray was convinced beyond a doubt that Benton's religion was real. One night at a prayer meeting held at Jake Benton's humble home, Mr. Gray became so convicted that resistance was impossible. He fully surrendered himself to Jesus and obtained an experience that was marvelous even in the eyes of Grandma Gray.

The news of Gray's conversion spread like fire on a dry prairie. He was a heavy contributor to the finances of Mount Olivet. On this account it became a matter of conjecture as to whether or not he would be excommunicated. However, Mr. Gray relieved all minds of any anxiety when on the following week he quietly withdrew his membership from the church.

The day following the night of Nolan Gray's conversion there occurred an incident that meant much to Jake Benton, as well as to Deacon Gramps. Benton was walking along the road that led around the fence from his own home to the large, white house occupied by Nolan Gray and his family. He was on his way to milk Mr. Gray's cow. He commonly went through the field on such occasions, as it was much the shorter route, but on this particular morning he had a mysterious disposition to take the long route around the road. When he had reached a point about a quarter of a mile from his home, to his astonishment he met Deacon Gramps, accompanied by Gramps' hired hand. He saw at once that the Deacon was in a most surly mood. So in a pleasant tone of voice Benton said, "Good morning, gentlemen, nice mornin'," aiming with salutation to pass on.

Gramps was not in any sense a brave man, as you may have guessed by this time, but he always manifested great boldness where he was sure there was no physical danger.

"They say Gray got your kind of religion at the prayer meetin' last night," he said.

"Well, I guess it ain't my kind," answered Benton, "but he sure did get Bible salvation."

Then the Deacon let loose in all his fury. "Jake Benton," said he, "this religion of yours has got to be stopped, it's got to be wiped out, it's doin' more harm in this community than all the saloons in the State. It's tearing up our church. Nolan Gray and old Grandma Gray was good church-members and have been for years and years and now they are taken in with this crazy holiness stuff, and you are the hul cause of it. I tell you it's just got to be stopped and I'm going' to stop it and I'll just begin right here." With this he advanced toward Benton and struck him a terrific blow on the side of the cheek with his open hand. At this Benton only replied, "God bless you, Mr. Gramps." This served only to incense the enraged Deacon all the more, and he literally flew at Benton and easily pinned him to the ground and sat upon his chest and beat him in the face most unmercifully. Poor Benton struggled and groaned, but did not endeavor to hurt his antagonist. The Deacon's hired hand was all his time a looker-on, but he finally mustered up courage, and with great difficulty succeeded in pulling the enraged Deacon off the poor man. When the hired man had finally persuaded Gramps away from the scene, Benton, bruised and bleeding in body, but victorious in soul, struggled to his feet and went home, glad that he was counted worthy to suffer for Jesus' sake.

CHAPTER VII

The community was stirred, no doubt about that. These were stirring days. Not since the days when Union and Southern marauding parties scattered terror in these woods had public excitement run so high as now. The gossip of Benton's beating was on everybody's lips before the sun went down that day. Everybody talked about it. Jake's friends were warmer friends and his enemies were hotter enemies. Those who had been neutral were neutral no more. There were just two parties now, those against and those for holiness as taught and lived by Jake Benton. As for old Jake, he kept sweet in his soul and talked little and prayed much. His victory was complete.

In the midst of this excitement Jake received a short but significant letter from Evangelist Blank. It ran thus:

Dear Brother Benton:

In accordance with my promise to you nearly a year ago, I am now in a position to hold your revival. I will arrive in Dobbinsville August 2. Please meet me at the train.

Your Brother in Christ,--Evangelist Blank.

Jake read this scanty letter through tears of joy. He was unspeakably happy. He had prayed for a year, and now his prayers were on the verge of being answered. A holiness preacher, mysterious being, was actually to set foot on Mount Olivet soil. The doctrine of full salvation was to invade the precincts of sin-you-must religion.

But where was Evangelist Blank to preach? Not in Mount Olivet, to be sure. About a quarter of a mile from Mount Olivet Church was a section of land known in that country as Public Land. Here in the center of an old, unused, unfenced field was a thick clump of post oak sapplings, with heavy foliage. This spot was to be the scene of many an interesting happening, a few of which shall be mentioned before this story closes and many of which shall not. As soon as Jake was sufficiently recovered from the beating administered by the Deacon, he, in company with Nolan Gray and several others who were either friends or embracers of the doctrine of full salvation, went to this spot and worked for a number of days building a brush arbor, which was to serve the purpose of a meeting-house. Long poles were tied from tree to tree to make a framework. Then other poles were laid across from the frame-poles to furnish a support for the brush, which was thrown on top. A sort of tabernacle was thus effected which served the purpose well. Oil torches were hung on the upright poles to furnish light. Long boards were brought from a sawmill near by and fastened on stakes driven into the ground; these served for benches. The arbor would seat about five hundred people.

Everything was in readiness for the long-expected meetings. All there was to do was to wait for the 2nd of August to come, and that was hard to do. Finally it came. That afternoon when the two-coached train rolled up to the little red station at Dobbinsville, Jake Benton stood on the depot platform. His heart beat a rat-a-tat-tat against his chest. As the train slowed up and Jake saw through its window the face of a man corresponding to the picture he had seen in his holiness paper, his emotions refused to yield to control. He jumped high in the air, and shouted at the top of his voice, "Hallelujah!"

The train being a few hours late, the afternoon was far spent. On the road from the station, Jake told Evangelist Blank as best he could of the happenings of the year just preceding--how he had been converted in the woods and subsequently sanctified, of his persecution and excommunication by the church, and of his recent beating at the hands of Deacon Gramps. Evangelist Blank had had many long years of experience in the field of evangelistic endeavor, yet when Jake Benton poured all these startling things into his ears, there came a feeling over him that he was entering into an entirely new experience. This feeling was verified before he left the neighborhood a few weeks later.

When the old-fashioned wagon rattled up to the front gate of the humble home, Evangelist Blank expressed to Jake the belief that in coming to this place he was in the center of the will of God. This made poor Jake's heart leap for joy. He sprang from the wagon to the ground and, bidding his good wife see to the comfort of the Evangelist and the corps of singers who accompanied him, set himself diligently to doing the evening chores in order that everything might be in readiness for the evening meeting.

CHAPTER VIII

When the afternoon shadows began to lengthen there began to gather around the new-made brush arbor on Post Oak Ridge a number of men and boys. These were mostly idlers of the community, who had nothing in particular to do, so had come early to the arbor. But when the last faint streaks of the dying day were fading, the more substantial citizens of the community began to gather at this spot of interest. They came from every direction. Every path seemed to lead to the arbor ridge. Some came in wagons, some in buggies, some on horseback, others walked.

Everybody, almost, was there. Grandma Gray was there. She sat serenely in her big willow rocker, which Nolan had placed just in front and to the left of the speaker's stand. Her age-wrinkled face was all aglow with the joy of full salvation. Aunt Sally Perkins was there. Poor old Aunt Sally. She was notorious as a shouter and a hypocrite. Nobody had any confidence in her as a Christian, but she was much given to sitting in the "amen" corner, and on this particular night she came into the big arbor and deposited her scanty self right on a front bench. And there she sat, wrapped in her old grey shawl, peeping out from beneath her old black bonnet. Old Brother Bunk was there. For a quarter of a century he had been a true and tried member of Mount Olivet Church, but of late he had been much wrought upon by the holiness agitation. "Spooky" Crane was there. Crane was a harmless half-wit who lived alone in a shanty at the back of Deacon Gramps' field. He always made it a point to attend every religious service far and near, of whatever faith, and he had the capacity for adjusting himself to his surroundings to such an extent that he joined every religious movement with which he came in contact. Roguish boys found great amusement in giving him pennies to sing for them. Jim Peabody was there. But that was to be taken only as a matter of course, for Jim always went to church. He went, not because he was religious, but because he was otherwise. He made loud boast of his infidelity. He had given himself extensively to the reading of Bob Ingersoll and other authors notorious for things other than goodness, so in his own vain imaginations he was a masterful scholar. He said there was no God, and that any man who prayed was a fool. But the cause of infidelity had suffered a terrific blow when one time Nolan Gray, as he was going to Dobbinsville, saw a huge wagon-box turned bottom side up, with the wagon on top, in a ditch by the side of the road. As he drew near he heard coming from under the box the low muttering tones of a man's voice. As he stood near the box and listened he heard a most eloquent prayer. He took a long pole from a fence near by and pried one edge of the box up, and who should emerge from beneath but Jim Peabody.

When the hour of service arrived, Jake Benton and the evangelistic party did not arrive with it. Owing to the lateness of the train, Jake had been unable to get around at the appointed hour. Finally the familiar rattle of Jake's wagon was heard, and now all was breathless expectancy. When the party arrived at the arbor, all eyes were fastened upon the Evangelist. If he had been a ghost moving about in the twilight of that summer evening, he would have been regarded with no more superstition by that rustic people. There was nothing whatsoever extraordinary in the physical appearance of Evangelist Blank. He was a man of average height and scant weight. His rather pallid face was covered with a scanty well-trimmed beard. His deep-set blue eyes sparkled with a pleasant earnestness. Any lack of physical attractiveness was amply atoned for by the splendid qualities of the man's soul. He was a mighty man of God. He had an unusual grip on the upper world. He had large capacities for moving God on his throne. A heavenly atmosphere pervaded the realm of his personality.

When this man stepped onto the platform of the large brush arbor that summer evening, and took his seat and faced that audience, there was a stillness that was painful. The awful stillness was broken when the Evangelist arose and said, "Praise God for his matchless salvation." He made a few preliminary remarks and the corp of singers began to sing. And such music seldom issues from human lips. It was not overwhelming in point of its artistic qualities. The compositions were of the simplest sort. But the singers sang from out of the abundance of redeemed souls, and there was a heavenly inspiration accompanying the songs that simply overwhelmed the hearts of sinners and overjoyed the hearts of saints. One song that especially gripped the audience ran thus:

"Do you triumph, O my brother, over all this world of sin?
In each storm of tribulation, does your Jesus reign within?"

CHORUS:

"I am reigning, sweetly reigning, far above this world of strife;
In my blessed, loving Savior, I am reigning in this life."

When this and several other hymns equally inspiring had been sung, Evangelist Blank arose and said, "Let us pray." At this the audience began to make arrangements to stand, for it was the custom in Mount Olivet Church in those days to stand while the preacher "made" his prayer, as

Deacon Gramps expressed it. But the Evangelist had the notion that when the heart is humbled before God the body should be in a like position, so he reverently and unpretentiously knelt beside the rough board pulpit. The four singers on the platform knelt simultaneously with the Evangelist. This placed the members of Mount Olivet in a rather embarrassing position. They disliked the idea of being so unreligious as to sit erect during prayer, and they could not bear the humiliation of kneeling at a holiness meeting. A few of them under the press of the circumstance did kneel. A few stood up. Most of them sat with bowed heads. "Spooky" Crane easily adjusted himself to the situation and promptly knelt in the straw, and with his face in his hands peeped between his fingers at the Evangelist. Jim Peabody, the infidel, sat arrogantly erect with an impish snarl on his lip. To him the whole business of praying was a huge piece of foolishness--except, of course, when under the wagon-box. Aunt Sally Perkins knelt beside the front bench and clapped her hands hysterically during the prayer. And Deacon Gramps had slipped under the outer edge of the arbor, where he sat on a low bench with his elbows on his knees and chewed his tobacco most vigorously.

Evangelist Blank, himself, led in prayer. His prayer, like himself, was simple, but mighty. It ran something like this:

"O Lord of heaven and earth, we thank thee for this hour. We have come here in thy name; we plead no worthiness and no efficiency of our own. Thy blood and thy grace is all our plea. We would not thrust ourselves into thy holy presence on any human merits. But in thy name and through the blood of Christ our Saviour we come boldly before thee. We praise thee, Lord, for thy great salvation, by which thou dost save us and sanctify us. O Lord, make thyself mighty in the salvation of this people among whom we have come to labor. Let thy matchless power be manifested and thy righteous name be exalted. Be thou lifted up before the people. Lord, we rededicate ourselves at this hour to be used of thee in the salvation of men. Come into these temples of clay afresh at this hour, O Lord, and let the fire of thy holy presence consume all the dross that may be in us. Anoint our feeble lips to speak the unsearchable riches of Christ ... Hear us, Lord, we ask in Jesus' name. Amen."

This prayer made a profound impression on the audience. When it was finished, a few other songs were sung, and then Evangelist Blank arose to address the audience. There was something about the preaching and personality of this man that made him a unique figure in the field of preacherdom. In the first place, he was masterful in his knowledge and use of the Holy Scriptures. He knew God's Book. By patient study and long practice he had brought himself to the place where he could readily bring to his defence an impregnable line of Scriptural proof to sustain the propositions that he held. He was not only proficient in the Scriptures, but he had a thorough training covering the whole range of ministerial and theological thought. He had the happy and unusual combination of those qualities of mind that make for forceful oratory and clearness in theological thought. And last, and far from least, he walked with God. He had a yearning for the lost of earth's millions.

On that evening when he faced for the first time his brush-arbor audience, it was plainly to be seen that he did not lack for something to say. He did not let his sermon get in the way of his message. He went right to the heart of his subject, which he announced as Salvation. He took for his text Titus 2:11, 12: "For the grace of God that bringeth salvation hath appeared to all men, teaching us that, denying ungodliness and worldly lusts, we should live soberly, righteously, and godly in this present world."

His sermon ran partly thus: "My friends and brethren, we are here this evening to conduct this service in the fear of God. Almost a year ago I received a letter from Brother Benton urging me to come to his place to hold a revival. Owing to my many calls, I was unable to come until the present time, and now at last we are here in the name of God. We expect him to give us a gracious out-pouring of his Holy Spirit. The text that I have read in your hearing introduces my subject, the subject of Salvation. I feel the burden of this message pressing upon my heart. Since Jesus saved me from a life of sin I have had a consuming desire to get others to press their way into this grand experience. I shall not promise to keep within the bounds of homiletical order tonight, but I do promise to keep within the bounds of God's Holy Word and the leadings of his Spirit." These introductory remarks were stated with a simple earnestness born of a desire to see men saved.

The Evangelist first proceeded to show what salvation is. He said it is a divine work of grace in the heart, wrought by the blood of Jesus Christ. He explained that it means deliverance from sin. He said that if the Bible teaches anything at all, it teaches that the individual must have a vital connection with Jesus Christ.

Next the Evangelist set forth the conditions of salvation. "First," he said, "a man must be sorry for his sins; secondly, he must repent of his sins; and, thirdly, he must forsake his sins."

He dwelt at great length on the effects of salvation in the heart. He said that if a man's religion did not have any effect on him, it was worthless. A man's religion must make him a new creature, he argued. He declared that salvation makes a man love even his enemies. He said salvation cleanses a man from inward and outward filth.

By the time Evangelist Blank had illustrated and amplified all his points he had consumed the major portion of an hour and a half of time. During this time the entire audience was held spellbound by his simple and earnest eloquence.

All this was strange theology to the members of Mount Olivet Church. It was a stinging rebuke to their crooked and hypocritical lives.

CHAPTER IX

It was about the fifth night of the big holiness meeting at the arbor on Post Oak Ridge. The country was stirred for miles around. People from Dobbinsville and Ridgetown and neighboring villages were in regular attendance. Scores of people had been converted. Many had been sanctified. Numbers had been healed. The forces of sin were enraged. Wicked men, grim with age, had melted like frost at noonday under the mighty preaching of the Spirit-filled Evangelist. Old women with lying hearts and gossiping lips had been stricken down in mighty and pungent conviction for their sins. Young men, roguish and rough and stout-hearted, had come to the old split-log altar and on penitent knees had sobbed out before God the awful sins of their hearts and had gone away happy with the new-found treasure of full salvation. Young ladies, vain and haughty, had melted under the gospel messages and had come to the feet of Jesus. Sweet children not yet in their teens had wept their childish transgressions away and in their simple faith had accepted Jesus as their Savior. Oh, grand and glorious gospel! How matchless is its power.

Well, as I said, it was about the fifth night of the meeting. Preacher Bonds was there, and had been the two nights preceding. He had regarded all the manifestations of God's power in the meetings with affected indifference. He said he hated holiness and would hate it as long as he lived. On being asked what he thought of the miraculous conversions that had taken place in the meeting, he remarked that he would not believe in holiness even if Beelzebub himself were converted in the meetings.

Evangelist Blank said he thought this would be a splendid time to have a testimony-meeting. So they had one, and he conducted it himself. Grandma Gray was the first to testify. She stood trembling, and balanced herself against the back of the old willow rocker. Around her saintly face there seemed to circle a halo of glory. At first she only stood and wept. When she had gained control of her emotions sufficiently to speak, she said, "Oh, the love of God is unspeakable. How can I praise him for what he has done for me? He saves me and sanctifies me and heals me. I praise him for sending Evangelist Blank here. I would not say a word against the people of Mount Olivet church, but for thirty-some years I lived in that church an up-and-down life. God knows I wanted to live for him all that time but my experience was not sufficient to keep me. But since I have learned of the more perfect way, how my heart rejoices in this full salvation. Since this meeting began, the good Lord has been showing me great light on the church question. I see the one body of Christ, which is the church. I have just learned that I was born into the real, true church thirty-some years ago. O brethren, the day is dawning, the light is shining. How glad I am that I have lived to see this day."

When Grandma Gray had well-nigh exhausted her feeble strength in exhorting the people to come to Jesus and accept his truth, she sank into her big willow chair and silently prayed. For a brief period there was a deathlike stillness over the audience.

For years Grandma Gray had lived a life that could not be gainsaid. True, she spoke in her testimony about her up-and-down life, but when compared with the average professed Christian's life in that community, hers was above reproach. In her extreme age she spoke as one from the border-lands of eternity, and her words naturally had a profound effect.

Jake Benton was next to testify. He was simply overwhelmed with joy, and spoke at some length of his hope of someday being reunited with his darling girl in the skies. Jake's testimony scattered enthusiasm all through the congregation of the saints and there was rejoicing and praising God that was doubtless participated in by the angels around the throne.

Little flaxen-haired Eva Gray, eleven-year-old daughter of Nolan Gray, arose and said that Jesus had saved her and that she aimed to spend her life for him, as had Grandma Gray. Thus we see a godly life is fruitful of influence even on the lives of little children.

Probably the most remarkable testimony given was that of Squire Branson. Branson spoke thus: "Friends and brothers: I stand before you a redeemed man. I am washed and made white in the blood of Jesus. I am as a brand snatched from the burning. I am now in my eighty-third year. You know the manner of my life up until this meeting. I have had absolutely nothing to do with religion. As you know I have lived a life of great wickedness. I have been a drunkard, a gambler--a mighty sinner. For fifty-three years I had not gone near a church service until this meeting began. I have been thoroughly put out with the type of Christianity exhibited in this community these past years. But when through sheer curiosity I came into this arbor, I was made as conscious of the presence of the Holy Ghost as if I could have seen him with my natural eyes. There at that altar night before last I unburdened my heart of the sins of nearly eighty years, and I stand tonight a witness of the redeeming grace and love of Christ my Saviour. Oh, how can I praise him enough? Here I stand right at the threshold of death with a long and wasted life behind me and an eternity of bliss before me. What but the mercy of an infinite God could bring about this wonderful change?"

"Spooky" Crane said in his testimony that of all the churches he had ever belonged to this one was the best. Aunt Sally Perkins shouted.

Evangelist Blank was just ready to close the meeting when he was interrupted by Preacher Bonds. Bonds' face was red with rage and his eyes gleaming with anger when he burst forth in this unceremonious manner; "I thank God for a sensible and reasonable religion. I have been a Christian for thirty years and a minister for twenty years and I have never experienced any of this wonderful joy that these people speak of. This sanctified holiness doctrine is the most damnable doctrine that ever struck this country, or any other country. I knew a group of these holiness people back in Kentucky where I came from. They said they could not sin and that they were just as good as Jesus Christ himself. They were given to all sorts of fanatical projects. They claimed to have great faith and went so far as to say they were healed, as some of these people have said tonight. One of them even said that by faith he had caused an iron wedge to float on the water. Talk about living free from sin. There never could be a more crooked doctrine preached. The Bible plainly says, 'There is none good, no not one.' It also says that 'If a man liveth and saith he sinneth not, he is a liar and the truth is not in him.' I believe the Bible. When I was in college old Professor Thorndike used to give us an occasional lecture on the Hellish Heresy of Holiness. He knew all about the doctrine and the harm it is doing these days. I am bold to say right here that God has called me and raised me up to fight holiness, and I have dedicated my life to this cause. I aim to use every means, fair and foul, to stamp this doctrine out of this community (Deacon Gramps, "Amen."). I want to warn Preacher Blank and every one of his dupes right here that if he continues to preach in this community he does so at his own peril. You people have no right, legal or moral, to come here and disturb the peace and tranquility of Mount Olivet church, a church that has stood standpat for nearly half a century in defence of the truth. I here and now call upon every loyal member to come to the defence of the faith of your fathers. Those who will pledge their united support to the cause of stamping out holiness rise to your feet."

At this a score and a half of rustic mountaineers boldly stood up. "Let those who have made this solemn pledge meet me at the back door of the arbor," said Bonds as he sat down.

CHAPTER X

During the time that Bonds was on the floor, Evangelist Blank leaned against the pulpit with his face in his hands as if in prayer. When Bonds sat down the Evangelist calmly faced the audience. Just at this time he seemed to possess the meekness of a lamb and the boldness of a lion. He seemed perfectly composed, as he remarked, "Well, brethren and friends, I am indeed sorry to see this splendid testimony meeting end in this way. I am sorry the ministerial brother feels as he does toward the truth we have preached, and I hope after prayer and reflection he will see his way clear not to hinder the progress of the meeting. However, if God sees fit to allow the hand of persecution to fall upon us, we bow submissively to his will. But we will not, we dare not compromise God's truth. We will preach the Bible regardless of consequences." With these remarks Evangelist Blank closed the service.

After the service was closed everything seemed to be as usual except for a few whisperings around in regard to what Preacher Bonds had said. As was usually the case at the close of such meetings, the saints gathered in little groups about the front end of the arbor and talked freely of their common faith and love. Mothers began to arouse sleepy-eyed children from their dreams and break to them the sad news that they were not at home in bed. Bushy-headed, bearded farmers and woodsmen began ramming their grimy hands into the hip pockets of their "blue drillin' overhauls," in which sequestered quarters were prone to hide their "long twist" and homemade cob pipes. After injecting an ample amount of "long twist" into the cob pipe's empty stomach and lighting a match thereto and sending a few initiatory puffs into the air, these mountaineers made off in the darkness toward their homes in different directions. Some went in groups, some by twos, some singly. Seen from a distance in the blackness of the night these companies resembled a regiment of glow-worms in a potato patch. From over the flint hills in the distance came the familiar rattle and rumble of old-fashioned lumber wagons whose occupants had come far to hear the much-discussed preacher from "over east." Now and then the night air was pierced by hideous yells and whistles from roguish boys dashing along on horseback, whose popularity depended on the amount of noise they made.

Is the offense of the cross ceased? Nay, verily; they that "live godly in Christ Jesus shall suffer persecution." So say the Scriptures, and so thought Evangelist Blank as he lay down to rest that night after he had closed the testimony-meeting. Evangelist Blank slept in a tent, which had been pitched near the brush arbor. Several such tents had been pitched by Jake Benton and other neighbors, who, finding it ill convenient to go to and from the meeting each night, had decided to run it somewhat on the camp-meeting plan.

On the particular night of which we have been speaking, Evangelist Blank from some cause unknown to him was awakened shortly after midnight. Not being able to resume sleep, he thought to improve even the midnight time by musing on the goodness of God. As he lay thus gazing through the thin canvas of his tent at the moon, which was now a two hour's journey in the sky, he was startled by the sight of a man's shadow on the side of the tent. He lay still and listened. Soon he heard low muttering voices a few rods from his tent. Still he listened. They drew nearer and nearer. Finally the mutterings became whisperings. Still he listened, and prayed. They came nearer. Soon several shadows were cast on the canvas. He saw the winding shadow of a rope as it dangled from the arms of one of the men. Still he listened. Still they whispered.

"No difference about Benton, we want the preacher," he heard one say.

"Are you sure this is his tent?" whispered another.

"Yes, I saw him sitting in this tent's door reading this afternoon," whispered a third.

"We must get the rope on him and make away with him before the camp is aroused," someone said.

"What shall I do?" thought the pious man. "Does it mean that I must suffer death at the hands of this mob, simply because I have preached the truth? Will they hang me? Will they choke me? Will they stone me? Will they drag me over these awful rocks until life is dashed out? What meant the gleam in Bonds' eyes last night in the service? What will become of my dear wife and boy in Ohio? Will I recant? Will I deny my Lord? Will I shun to declare the whole counsel of God?" All these questions and many others flashed across the Evangelist's mind like angry streaks of lightning across a black cloud.

Through the thin canvas he saw in the moonlight half a dozen husky men seize hold of one end of a rope, the other end of which was arranged in a slip-loop.

"Now when I get the rope on him, make for the hills," said one man as he began to untie the strings that held the door of the tent. Just at this instant Evangelist Blank slipped under the edge of the tent on the opposite side from where the men were planning their diabolical feat, and under the edge of Jake Benton's tent, which stood just about two feet from his own. With a quickness of mind that was almost miraculous, he donned a dress and shawl and bonnet belonging to Sister Benton, and stole out of the tent and across the ground toward the arbor in full view of the enraged men as they came out of the tent that he had just vacated.

The men were as much astonished as enraged at not finding their prey. They ransacked Jake Benton's tent and demanded that he reveal the whereabouts of the preacher. Jake flatly refused. Except for his trembling, he stood like a stone wall and faced that score of masked men, thirsty for righteous blood. Really they appeared as so many thoroughbred devils right from the pit. They were masked in a way, not only to conceal their identity, but in a way to make them appear as hideous as possible. The leader of the mob shouted, "Jake Benton, you sanctified hypocrite, if you don't tell us where that preacher is we'll hang your carcass up for the crows to pick."

"Maybe you will, but I'll hang there, before I'll tell," shouted poor Jake in a trembling voice.

"Who was that ole lady left your tent and went across the ground a while ago with a bonnet on?" shouted one of the mob.

"I never saw an ole lady going across the ground," replied Jake. (In this he was telling the truth, you know.)

"Hang him up to a tree boys, hang him up, if he won't tell," shouted one of the gang. "Bring the rope," shouted another as he took hold of Benton's arms.

Just at this juncture the leader of the mob suggested to Jake that if he and his comrades would break up camp and leave the ground immediately, they would not hang him, but would continue their search for the Evangelist. To this Jake and the whole party of campers readily agreed. In the light of the moon, the whole ground of campers, consisting of more than a dozen families, hitched their teams to their wagons and made their way over the hills homeward. Before any wagon was allowed to leave the ground, it was carefully searched by the mob to ascertain whether or not Evangelist Blank were there. He could not be found.

When old Brother Bunk and his family arrived at their home, which was two miles from the campground. Sister Bunk and the Bunk children were afraid to go into the house until Brother Bunk should unharness the team and go with them. When the Bunk family came to the yard, they were astonished to see in the moonlight somebody sitting under the old silver poplar-tree. They were scared to say the least. Sister Bunk and the Bunk children hovered closer and closer to Brother Bunk, while fear increased as the distance to the poplar-tree decreased. Imagine their surprise and relief when the person under the tree shouted, "Praise God, Brother Bunk, many are the afflictions of the righteous, but the Lord delivereth them out of them all." It was Evangelist Blank. He explained to them that he had walked the whole two miles from the camp through the woods, guided by the sound of the wagon, thus avoiding the possibility of being apprehended by the mob in case they should attack the wagon. He had arrived at the Bunk farm about the same time as the wagon had, but not having the inconvenience of a team to attend to, had sat down under the tree to rest.

The mob naturally supposed that Evangelist Blank would somehow make his way from the campground to Jake Benton's. Benton and his family arrived home from the camp about three o'clock in the morning. They had been there only half an hour when they were aroused by the shout of the mob, who demanded that the preacher should be yielded up to them. Not until they had thoroughly searched Benton's home would they believe Jake's contention that Evangelist Blank was not on the premises. Finally, when they were convinced that Benton could not or would not tell them where the preacher was they withdrew to a clump of woods a short distance from Benton's home and, the morning air being chilly, built a fire.

It was here that their identity became known. As they chatted around the fire they removed the masks from their faces. Of course, Jake Benton was curious to know who they were, and when he saw their fire in the woods he resolved to find out, even at the expense of much trembling. He thought he had recognized some of them by their voices when they talked to him at the camp, but now he determined to make sure. He crawled on his hands and knees for nearly a quarter of a mile along an old rail fence until he came within a distance of twenty rods from where the men were gathered, Indian fashion, around the fire. He was not at all surprised when he saw in the group the familiar face of Deacon Cramps and Reverend Bonds. And he observed from certain parts of their masks which they still had on that these two men were the fellows who took the leading part in the affair at the camp. Jake recognized that the group was made up mostly of men who were prominent members of Mount Olivet church. A few non-church-members and young men of the baser sort were also in the group. Benton watched them until nearly daybreak, when they disbanded and started for home. Jake lay quietly in his clump of buck-brush until he was sure that they were at a safe distance, then he crawled out and went home, informed much and scared more.

Shortly after sunrise, old Brother Bunk came over to tell Benton that Evangelist Blank was at his house safe, and happy in the Lord. This news greatly relieved Benton and his good wife, for they had not seen the Evangelist since he left their tent during the night, and they did not know just how he was faring. Evangelist Blank had suggested that it be announced that as this was Sunday there would be services held that day at Old Brother Bunk's. This idea pleased Benton, and he joined Brother Bunk in scattering the news among the saints. Accordingly at eleven o'clock the saints gathered at the Bunk home, where a blessed meeting was held. Great power and victory prevailed. The awful persecution had driven the saints to their knees in prayer. The very atmosphere round about seemed to be charged with the Holy Spirit's power. Evangelist Blank started to preach, but found it impossible. The saints shouted him down. A number of sinners who were present melted under the influence of the Holy Spirit and yielded their hearts to God. "Great grace was upon them all."

That night the meeting at the arbor was resumed, and it continued for two weeks with greater victory and power than before the molestation. The mob never bothered again, and the reason was this: A dozen or more men in the community who were sinners, and professed to be sinners, but who believed that men should be allowed to serve God according to the dictates of their own consciences, simply made it plain that the first fellows masked or unmasked who should disturb the meeting would be dealt with in a most uncomplimentary manner. The mob saw the situation in its true light and decided that for their own safety they would stay away.

When the meeting finally ran its natural course and came to a close, Evangelist Blank bade the band of saints a loving and tearful farewell and betook himself to other fields to suffer and rejoice in the great work with which God had entrusted him.

CHAPTER XI

Five years had flitted by since Jake Benton was converted down in the hills. The battle between holiness and sin-you-must religion had waxed hotter and hotter. Masked mobs had scoured the country at different times, threatening the very lives of enemies. The sin-you-must group had decreased in number, but had increased in wickedness. It could truthfully be said that every member of Mount Olivet church was at this time a positive force for evil. The membership had dwindled to one-fourth its former size. Somebody is responsible for the statement that the blackest deeds known to the world have been done in the name of religion, love, and liberty. Mount Olivet Church did her blackest deeds in the name of religion. She was determined to crush her adversaries, and she was not particular as to the means she used. Every member who had even the tiniest spark of God's love in his heart had either cast his lot with the holiness movement or given up his religious profession altogether. Preacher Bonds had grown more and more zealous in his fight against holiness.

Deacon Gramps had preached his doctrine everywhere, in his home as well as in the church, and he had already seen its fruits manifested right in his home. One of his sons who had now become of age had built a sort of philosophy of life on his father's teaching. He had reasoned something like this: "Since Father sins, and Mother sins, and the preacher sins, and everybody else sins, and nobody can keep from sinning, then it follows that one is not responsible for the sins he commits whether they be large or small, few or many. Then why not have a good time in this life? Why not go the full length into sinful pleasure?" And go the full length he did. He had become involved in one criminal scrape after another, and he would have landed in the penitentiary before this time had it not been for Deacon Cramps' financial backing. And by this time it had come to be common knowledge in the community that the son's profligacy was almost certain to involve the Deacon in financial ruin. It was a fact much discussed in inner business circles at Dobbinsville that Mr. Gramps' farm was heavily mortgaged, and that unless some crook or turn unforeseen favored him he would soon face bankruptcy. He had been unable to pay the interest on the notes he had been obliged to obtain in order to keep his son from going where he really belonged.

As for Jake Benton, during these five years since his conversion, his poverty had stuck closer to him than a brother; but thanks be to his persecutions, he had grown immensely rich in spiritual resources. He had become a mighty man in prayer. The sick were healed in answer to his prayer of simple faith. And it seemed only a natural thing for him to pray for his enemies. And as for love, Jake loved everybody and everybody had found it out. If anybody in the community wanted a favor done them, all that was necessary was to mistreat Benton and he would do them a favor. He had also developed into quite a preacher. Ever since the meeting closed in the brush arbor he regularly gathered the saints together on Sunday in the school house, and encouraged them in the things of the Lord. His life was simply exemplary, and even his bitterest enemies were compelled to acknowledge that God was with him.

One Sunday morning when Preacher Bonds stood before his meager audience, the familiar face of Deacon Gramps was absent. His unusual absence from the Church was very noticeable, and Preacher Bonds suggested in the introductory remarks of his sermon that unquestionably Brother Gramps was sick, and that it would be an act of brotherly kindness if when the service was over a number of the members would call at the Gramps' home and see the sick brother.

When Preacher Bonds had finished his sermon, a song had been sung, and the benediction had been invoked, a dozen or more of the members with Bonds in the lead started for the Gramps' home, which, as will be remembered, was plainly visible from the church.

"I believe," said Bonds, "that Brother Gramps' barn is on fire." At this the whole group began to rush toward the beautiful red barn that stood a quarter of a mile away. By the time they reached the spot, black clouds of smoke and angry flames were shooting from doors and cracks in the barn. Mrs. Gramps and the three children who were still at home were in the barnyard wringing their hands and crying in a heart-rending manner. It was plainly to be seen that the visitors could do nothing to save the barn, and all that remained to do was to stand and watch the flames devour the building.

"Where is Brother Gramps?" said Preacher Bonds to Mrs. Gramps.

"Wasn't he at church? No? Well, I don't know where he can be. He left the house just at church-time and I hadn't noticed but what he was in the crowd that came from the church," she replied.

Preacher Bonds looked serious as he said, "He could not have been in the barn, I suppose."

"Oh, certainly not. I suppose he must be at some of the neighbors', perhaps Deacon Brown's--was Deacon Brown at church?" "No, Deacon Brown was not at church," replied Bonds. "Possibly he remained at home and Brother Gramps went to see him on some business pertaining to the church. But I don't understand why they did not meet at the church to transact their business. Brother Jones, will you run over to Deacon Brown's and tell Brother Gramps about his awful accident?"

"Certainly," responded Jones, who stood near the barnyard gate talking with Gramps' hired hand, from whom he was endeavoring to learn the details as to how the fire started.

"Try to tell him," remarked Bonds, "in a way that will not be too much of a shock to him."

Jones mounted a horse and hurried off to Deacon Brown's and was soon back with the news that Gramps had not been seen at Brown's, and that Brown was sick in bed, which fact accounted for his being absent from the service that morning.

When it was learned that Gramps was not at Deacon Brown's, considerable anxiety began to be manifested on the part of neighbors. Some suggested that it was possible that Gramps could have been in the barn when it burned. Of course, care was exercised that such remarks should not reach the ears of Mrs. Gramps. Messages were sent to all the neighbors in search of Gramps. Someone had the idea that possibly he had gone to Dobbinsville or Ridgetown, but searchers sent to these places reported that he had not been seen at either place for several days. Preacher Bonds consoled Mrs. Gramps with the suggestion that doubtless he would show up before night. However, when night came with no signs of Deacon Gramps the whole community took an attitude of real alarm as to the likelihood that he had been burned to death. It was announced that there would be no meeting services at Mount Olivet Church, and Jake Benton dismissed his services and joined heartily in the search for the Deacon, who had dealt him so many grievous blows while Mrs. Benton did everything in her power to console Mrs. Gramps.

The search continued all through the night with no results. By early Monday morning there was general excitement for miles around. Scores of people came that morning from Dobbinsville and Ridgetown, and gazed on the mysterious scene of the former beautiful barn, now an ash heap. Officers came down from the county-seat and joined in the search for the lost Deacon. About the middle of the afternoon on Monday it was decided that the ash-heap should be searched for any evidence that the man had burned with the barn This search had not gone far when the county sheriff found in the ashes the steel back-springs and blades of a pocket-knife. Near by were found some pieces of enamel resembling a man's teeth. Next was found a small melted mass of something which seemed to have been a suspender buckle. Preacher Bonds picked up three pieces of silver which proved to have been so many silver dollars. Several pieces of bones were found, but these were so nearly charred to dust that it was impossible to determine whether they were bones of a man or bones of some of the many animals that perished with the building. However, all these articles mentioned were found within a very close proximity to each other, and in the minds of most people present there was now no doubt as to the fate of Deacon Gramps. On Monday night the coroner rendered a verdict that the Deacon met his death by being accidentally burned to death. Mrs. Gramps swooned away and had to have the attention of old Doctor Greenwich from Dobbinsville. In the event of the illness of Mrs. Gramps, it devolved upon Preacher Bonds to make full arrangements for the funeral, in which affair Jake Benton and his good wife showed every disposition to help where help was possible.

Preacher Bonds went to Dobbinsville and sent a telegram to each of the Deacon's five sons, two of whom lived in St. Louis, and three in Chicago. He also sent a telegram to a minister in St. Louis to come to preach the funeral, as, he said, he did not feel that he could officiate at the funeral of such a worthy brother as the departed. This St. Louis preacher had been a college chum of Preacher Bonds, and was full of the Mount Olivet persuasion.

Those were in the days before undertakers and other such modern conveniences had been introduced into that country. Jake Benton, good soul, went to Dobbinsville after the coffin and hauled it back in the same old lumber wagon he had hauled Evangelist Blank in five years before.

The funeral was arranged for Wednesday afternoon at two o'clock. A handful of ashes, together with the pocket-knife and other articles found in the ash-heap, was taken and wrapped in a napkin and placed in the big new coffin.

On Wednesday afternoon, when two o'clock arrived, the two front rooms of the Gramps farmhouse were crammed full of people. The yard was full, too. The St. Louis preacher began and spoke thus: "My friends and brethren, we have met on this sad occasion to pay our last respects to the honored dead. Within the narrow confines of this casket lie the earthly remains of a man whose spirit yet lives. It was not my happy privilege to know this excellent man, but I am informed by his pastor, Preacher Bonds here, of his manifold excellencies. When a great man dies, the people mourn. I am informed that our departed brother was a great man. First, he was a great man in business. When I behold this beautiful well-kept farm,

I see its wide, extending fields, its running brooks, its whitewashed fences, its excellent buildings, in the burning of one of which our brother met his death--when I behold these things, I say, I am made to exclaim that God hath blessed him in basket and store. Yes, a great man in business.

"Secondly, he was a great man in his home, and by the way, there is where the true greatness of a man is tested. In the death of our esteemed brother the home is the loser. It loses a loving husband. It loses a considerate father and an efficient bread-winner.

"Thirdly, our brother was a great man in the community. I am told that he was a public-spirited man. He believed in schools, in good roads, and in all other things that make for the welfare of a community. In his death the community is a heavy loser.

"Fourthly, he was a great man in the church. (Preacher Bonds, "Amen".) I am told that for upwards of thirty years our brother has been a consistent member of Mount Olivet Church and a regular attendant at its service and a heavy contributor to its funds. I understand that he was a mighty defender of the church's faith. He fought bravely on. He stood like a rock. He weathered the storm. He finished the course. He conquered.

"But, my friends, our finite minds cannot fathom the profound mysteries of the infinite. We cannot understand. Why would a just God permit such a noble man to meet such a tragic death? It is not ours to reason why. We simply bow our hearts to the will of the divine."

"And now, to the bereaved I would say, Weep not as those who have no hope. (Mrs. Gramps weeps aloud.) Brother Gramps is just gone on before. He has crossed over Jordan, where he waits on the sunny banks of sweet deliverance. Just a few more days and we shall join him. He has gone where the wicked cease from troubling and the weary be at rest. Let us pray. Brother Bonds, lead us."

CHAPTER XII

Twelve moons had rolled by since the Gramps funeral. The blue-grass sod had already grown quite snugly over the year-old mound in the cemetery back of the white church on the hill. The rose-bush at the head of the mound had bloomed once and the June breeze had sprinkled its pink petals over the green carpet. A more or less expensive tombstone stood modestly at the head of the mound and silently announced to the passer-by what any tombstone is supposed to announce, namely that somebody sleeps beneath this mound. During the year many persons had stood with bared heads and read through tears this inscription: J.D. Gramps, Born April 21, 1856--Died June 13, 18--. "They rest from their labors; and their works do follow them."

The Gramps premises began to show signs of decay. The fences were in need of repair and the hillside portions of the farm had been washed in gullies by the spring freshets. A large ash-heap surrounded by jimsonweed and burdock marked the sight of the once beautiful red barn. The front-yard gate had been torn from its hinges, and it lay upon the ground.

It was well known that Widow Gramps had received ten thousand dollars from an insurance company in New York City, but what she had done with the amount was only a matter of opinion. Along about this time it became known in the community that the Widow had leased the farm and was planning to go to a Western State as she said, for the sake of her health, which had been declining since the day of the Deacon's funeral.

One day when Mrs. Gramps was in Dobbinsville making preparations for the trip West, she called at the People's State Bank and presented a check drawn on a Western bank and signed by James Duncan. When the cashier had cashed her check and she had left the bank, he turned to his assistant and said, "Jim, do you know what Deacon Gramps' name was?"

"J.D. Gramps," responded the assistant.

"I know J.D. were his initials," said the cashier, "but what does J.D. stand for?"

"Oh, I don't remember," answered the assistant. "I suppose we could find out by looking up some of his old papers that we still have in the vault."

"Look up that old mortgage that Gramps had on the Widow Smith's little farm," ordered the cashier.

A ponderous file was pulled from a shelf in the vault and the two men began to search the musty and dusty old documents of bygone days. At last they found the mortgage. There they found the Deacon's name written out in full--James Duncan Gramps. The cashier of the People's State Bank had a curious twinkle in his eye as he looked at his assistant. "Jim, do you know, I have a suspicious feeling about this here Gramps proposition," he remarked. The assistant looked astonished. He had supposed all this time that the cashier was interested in the Deacon's full name from some official standpoint. The cashier went on: "Widow Gramps was just in here a few minutes ago and cashed a check drawn by a man by the name of James Duncan. I have a suspicion that Deacon Gramps is still living and that this James Duncan is no other than James Duncan Gramps, and he is checking out of a Western bank money which Mrs. Gramps received from the insurance company in New York."

"Surely that could not be," responded the assistant. "Suppose we compare the handwriting on the check that you just cashed with the handwriting on these old papers." After a close comparison of the two specimens of handwriting, the men decided that their resemblance was not sufficient to prove anything.

"At any rate it will do no harm to investigate," remarked the cashier as he closed the heavy door of the vault. "I shall turn the evidence over to the insurance company in New York." That evening at sundown when train Number 29 pulled out from the station at Dobbinsville and sped eastward, it carried in its mailcoach a letter of much significance addressed to the president of a large insurance company in New York City.

The following week one day when the west-bound noon train stopped at Dobbinsville, a well-dressed stranger stepped from the platform of the coach and made inquiry as to the location of a hotel. A lanky-looking lad who leaned against a pole directed the stranger to the Dobbinsville Inn, across the street. A person of this man's evident rank and importance was not a familiar sight in the streets of Dobbinsville. His mysterious presence set a peaceful town all agog. He became the subject of much exaggerated conjecture. Every fellow was overly eager to tell precisely what he did not know; namely, where this stranger came from and what his business was. Uncle Hezekiah Evans, the sixty-year-old newsboy who peddled the Post around over the village, said this stranger was evidently a rich man from the East who had come to buy the whole town out. "Fatty" Jones, whose chief employment was that of sitting on a baggage truck at the depot, had the opinion that this stranger was the son of a St. Louis millionaire who, having much time and money, had come out to an up-to-date country to spend both. It was the candid opinion of old "Doc" Greenwich that this stranger had committed a crime somewhere and was lounging around in this secluded nook to evade the officers of the law. "Dad" Brunt, the honored proprietor of the Dobbinsville Inn, had an advantage over his fellows, as the stranger was staying with him. He was sure that this man was interested in timberlands in the Mount Olivet neighborhood, as he had known the man to make two trips out here during his stay at the Inn.

The stranger spent a week in Dobbinsville, during which time he made frequent calls at the People's State Bank. When he had gone, the cashier, to the great relief and surprise of his fellow townsmen, explained to them that he was an officer of the law whose business was to investigate the circumstances connected with the burning of Deacon Gramps' barn.

Just about one month from this time Uncle Hezekiah Evans did a flourishing business selling papers. The Post came out with this startling headline: "DEACON HEARS OWN FUNERAL PREACHED." Great excitement prevailed. Everybody in Dobbinsville who could read and some who could not bought a paper from Uncle Hezekiah. He sold all he had, and wished for more to sell. Not only were the people of Dobbinsville interested in this remarkable newspaper headline, but in every town and city that fell within the limits of the Post's rather metropolitan circulation, people were startled at the unusual thought of a man hearing his own funeral. The article in the Post read like this:

The little town of Dobbinsville, snugly tucked away in the peaceful folds of the far-famed Ozark hills, is coming into its share of publicity. There has lived for many years in the vicinity of this village a substantial farmer by the name of Gramps. Until a couple of days ago Gramps was supposed to have been dead and buried. In fact, a tombstone in the churchyard near the Gramps homestead plainly states that Gramps is dead. Though tombstones sometimes say, "They have gone to rest," the truth is otherwise and Gramps has turned up very much alive. According to an officer interviewed by a Post correspondent yesterday, Gramp's story is somewhat on this wise:

A little over a year ago it became known in the neighborhood of Dobbinsville that Gramps, who for years had been a well-to-do farmer and a diligent deacon in a local church, was becoming involved in financial embarrassment. In order to save himself from bankruptcy, the Deacon, according to his own confession, resorted to very unusual means. Gramps carried heavy life insurance. About thirteen months ago he burned his barn and feigned to have burned with it. While his neighbors were at the church one Sunday he went into his big barn and after depositing in a pasteboard box his false teeth, his watch, his pocket-knife, and some pieces of silver coin, he placed the box in the manger and lighted the hay in the mow with a match. After making sure that the fire was in good way, he jumped from a window in the barn and ran, without detection, to his house and hid himself in the attic. Neighbors, missing Gramps, made a diligent search for him which resulted only in finding the molten remains of the pocket knife and other articles in the ash-heap where the barn was burned. Amid much mourning loving hands gathered ashes from the tragical spot and tenderly laid them in an expensive casket. The next day at the funeral in the parlor of the Gramps home, a minister from St. Louis delivered an empassioned eulogy, extolling the manifold excellencies of the honored dead (?). Through an open stairway door Gramps heard the eloquent words of the clergyman and the heart-rending sobs of his own wife and children.

After seeing his funeral done up in proper style, Gramps went to Colorado, where for a year, going under an assumed name, he conducted a Sunday School and took active part in other religious enterprises. Through the cooperation of his wife, who remained on the homestead at Dobbinsville, he came into possession of $10,000 from an insurance company in New York City. At the end of a year he planned for his wife to join him in Colorado, where, according to his statement, they were to begin life anew. But their plans were upset when the Deacon sent his wife a check signed with his assumed name, which name consisted of the first two words of his real name. Gramps and his wife are both in jail, where they await the action of the court and where they have a splendid opportunity to meditate upon the interesting happenings of the past year. Whether or not Mrs. Gramps was an accomplice has not yet developed.

CHAPTER XIII

"Twenty years ago I came to this country. During these twenty years I have done my utmost to preserve and defend the faith of Mount Olivet church." The person who spoke was Preacher Bonds. The place where he spoke was in his own pulpit. The persons to whom he spoke were his twenty members, who were the fragments of the once thriving and powerful rural church. Bonds was at his best on this particular Sunday morning in April, and he had planned to give his hearers a sort of history of the events during his twenty-years pastorate at Mount Olivet.

The morning was a most beautiful one. All nature wore a smile. Only those who have experienced the rare joy of taking a stroll through the wooded dell in the famous Ozarks on a spring morning can fully appreciate the scene. Spring had made her long-delayed journey from the southland and by the strength of her warm and winning ways had forced grim old winter to a hasty retreat northward, and now exulted in her unchallenged sway. All the birds on this morning seemed to have come out to help her in her celebration. A red-bird, perched on the tip-top twig of the venerable oak which stood near the church, bathing his crimson feathers in the morning sun, warbled his sweetest notes to his mate in a hawthorn thicket across the field. Rollicking robins were vying with each other in their quest of worms in the meadow east of the church. A gray squirrel chattered in a hickory-tree near by and scattered particles of bark all around. A red-headed woodpecker sat in the round door of his cozy house in an old snag and seemed perfectly content in his utter inability to sing. Frolicsome spring lambs amused themselves by butting each other off a low stump down in the old Gramps cow pasture.

The Church itself showed signs of dilapidation. The belfry on the roof had been torn away and the old rusty bell, silent for many years, stood exposed to the ravages of summer and winter. Its only purpose now seemed to be to afford a shelter for the wasps which from year to year built their nests in its dome. The brick chimney, which projected from the roof near the rear of the building, had lost its crowning bricks and presented a very jagged aspect. For the accommodation of the squirrels who were accustomed to take up winter quarters in the attic of the church, the wood-peckers had pecked numerous holes in the paintless walls. The eaves were daubed with mud carried by the pewees in the building of their yearly nests. Bats, at their own good pleasure, came in and out through the paneless windowsashes and found daytime repose on top of the sagging beam which, just above the windows, spanned the room.

The physical condition of this Church house formed a fitting counterpart to the spiritual condition of the people who worshipped (?) there. Physical, spiritual, and moral spelled the trinity of its decay.

Preacher Bonds' sermon that morning ran something like this: "Twenty years ago I came to this country. Well do I remember the first few months after landing here. Some of the older members will recall the mighty religious fight that was just beginning in those days between the holiness heresy and the doctrines of the Bible as believed in by this church. Those few who are here this morning who have known me and have been my co-workers throughout these years, I am sure, testify to the steadfastness with which I have stood by the work. I said when I came here that God had sent me here to fight the doctrine of holiness. I still hold to my mission. I have stood four-square against that doctrine and all its advocates, and I still stand. I have used every means to put it down. But strange as it seems, this heresy appears to have grown fat upon our opposition, and the more we have fought the more it has flourished. Even at this very hour not a mile from here, in the schoolhouse, there is a group of people five times as large as this audience worshipping the Lord in what they call the "beauty of holiness." They have for a preacher, as you know, old man Benton, who twenty years ago was cast out of this church for teaching crooked doctrine. He has had no preparation whatever for ministerial work, but in some way he has been able to keep his bunch together for nearly twenty years; and now since he is an old man, it seems that they still persist in following him.

"In the early days of my pastorate here my strongest supporter and co-laborer was Deacon Gramps. This name will sound familiar to some of the older members. Gramps owned the beautiful farm just to the west of this Church. A good many years ago through some play, fair or foul, Gramps was charged with a criminal act and was convicted and sent to the penitentiary, where three years ago he died. His wife went to St. Louis to live with her son, and departed this life shortly after moving there. You are all more or less familiar with the Gramps story, so I shall leave it, as it is not at all a pleasant topic to discuss.

It may be of interest to some of you to know just how the doctrine of holiness ever got started in this community. Well, this old man Benton whom you all know as the leader of the holiness movement used to be a member of this church. For many years he lived a consistent Christian life in this church, so they tell me. About twenty years ago he spent a whole summer herding cattle down in the hills about thirty miles from here. While he was down there in the woods all alone with nothing to occupy his mind, he fell to musing on the death of his little girl who died a good many years previously to that time and it seems that he became mentally unbalanced, at least on religious matters. According to the information given me, he came in contact at this time with a religious paper teaching strange doctrines, and he embraced these doctrines and began advocating them with great zeal. As I said before, he was excommunicated from this church for teaching such doctrines, but in leaving the church he took a number of our most trusted and tried members, for instance, the Gray family. Those were the days of great excitement in this community. It was about this time that I was called to the pastorate of this church. A few months after my coming Benton and his bunch got an evangelist from over east, somewhere, to come here, and he made a mighty stir along heretical lines and many of the best citizens of our community were drawn into the delusive net. Some of us, in those days, stood firm in the faith and employed every thinkable means to stamp out the nefarious cult; and allow me to humbly say that had it not been for Deacon Gramps and me and a few other faithful ones, our cause at that time would have been completely lost.

"But I stand today, my brethren, as I have always stood--unalterably opposed to the program of the holiness movement. First, I oppose holiness itself--the doctrine that a man can live free from sin in this life. How foolish, how utterly ridiculous, the idea. We all sin. Our fathers sinned, we sin, and our posterity will sin. Do you see that streak of sunshine that comes in at the window and falls upon the floor? See in the sunlighted atmosphere a million dust particles. Let the air represent our lives and let the dust particles represent our sins, and you will have an idea as to how many sins we commit. Away with the holiness doctrine.

"Secondly, I stand opposed to the doctrine of divine healing as taught by Benton's outfit. The days of miracles are past. They ceased with the apostles. Jesus Christ has no more power to heal me of sickness today than has the horse which I rode to church this morning. In these days of great learning, when men are able to cure diseases by medicine and surgery, there is no need of divine healing, and every man who claims to be healed by divine power makes himself an ignoramus and a liar. Away with this doctrine.

"Thirdly, I stand opposed to the doctrine of oneness, or unity, as taught by Benton and his disciples. They lay great stress on this doctrine. They say there is but one church and that when a man is converted he becomes a member of this one church. Brethren, I do not believe this new doctrine. I still hold to the faith of our fathers. I believe that according to the Scriptures we become members of the church by water baptism and by no other method.

"Brethren, let us stand by the faith of those who have gone before. We may be few in number, but let us be unmovable. Let us refresh our faith with thoughts of those whose lives have left sacred spots on the field of memory. Let us think on such men as Preacher Crookshank and Deacon Gramps, who were noted for their courage in defending the faith.

"As the noon hour is drawing near, I must bring my sermon to a close. Tonight at seven-thirty I shall preach on a favorite subject of mine--the Hellish Heresy of Holiness. But, in conclusion, let me say that I still feel heavily the burden of fighting old man Benton and his group. I am growing somewhat gray, but I'm still in the fight. I aim to push the battle. I believe that in defending his faith a man is justifiable in using almost any means imaginable. Let us pray: Lord, we thank thee for this hour in which we have defended thy cause. Lord, bless this church and curse those who seek its harm. Smite any person or persons in this community who seek to propagate false religion. And now may the grace of Jesus Christ, and the love of God, and the communion of the Holy Ghost rest and abide with us now and forever, amen."

So closed a service a picture of which today still hangs on the walls of the memory of those present.

How hidden is the path of one's future. When Preacher Bonds mounted his sorrel horse at the church that noon-day, just as he had done for many, many years, little did he think that the same sun which afforded him a chance to illustrate in his morning sermon the multiplicity of his own sins would, before setting that day, shine upon his lifeless form.

It so happened that day that Preacher Bonds invited one of his brethren home with him to dinner. As he and this member, who was a pillar in the church, rode along the country road to Bonds' home, Bonds gave the member a full outline of his intended sermon on the Hellish Heresy of Holiness. When the two men had reached the barn of the Bonds' premises and had fed their horses they started for the house. They were just passing in at the yard gate when Preacher Bonds staggered and fell to the ground. He was carried into his house and placed on a cot, and a doctor was called; but within a half-hour from the time he fell at the gate his breath ceased and he began his eternity. The doctor pronounced his death due to heart trouble. There was no sermon at the church that night on the Hellish Heresy of Holiness. The following day Bonds' remains were started on the journey to Kentucky, where burial took place at the old boyhood home.

With the passing of Bonds the last candlestick was removed from Mount Olivet church. Bonds' sermon was the last one of the sin-you-must type preached there. The church was entirely disbanded and the dilapidated building finally fell into the hands of those who came after Jake Benton. In recent years the old church has been torn away and replaced by a beautiful white building surpassing even the former beauty of the old one. Over its door were written these words: The Church of God--the Pillar and Ground of the Truth. Over the pulpit this motto hangs: "Behold how good and how pleasant for brethren to dwell together in unity." To the left on the wall are these words: "Who forgiveth all our iniquities and healeth all our diseases."

CHAPTER XIV

Harry Benton was a successful business man, there was no question about that. He was not known in the commercial world as a "big" man, and he could not write out a check for a million dollars and give it to some charitable institution as some of the multi-millionaires can do, but he was regarded by all who knew him as a successful business man. He had a business in Chicago that was thriving if not colossal. From the income from this business he was able to own and maintain a beautiful and comfortable home in one of the residential districts of the great city. It was his pleasure and privilege to give each year a few thousand dollars to the cause of the gospel of Jesus Christ.

Harry was the second son of Jake Benton, the backwoods holiness preacher of the Ozarks. At the age of twenty-one he had become the husband of Eva Gray, who was two years younger than he. This union had been a blessed happy one. If all of Chicago's homes were like that of Harry Benton, it might well be nicknamed the Paradise of America. Thrice the angel of blessings had visited this home, decorating it each time with one of heaven's jewels in the form of a baby. Nolan Benton, the twelve-year-old boy, had the name of his Grandfather Gray, and he also had all the religious indications of his Grandfather Benton. Blanche was two years younger than Nolan. She fell heir to the blue eyes, the ruddy cheeks, the flaxen hair of her mother. Little Jake, the baby, was five years old. He inherited his Grandfather Benton's name and his Grandfather Gray's red hair.

One Sunday morning when this happy family gathered around the breakfast table, Harry Benton's appetite was absent. He could not eat. He steadfastly gazed through the east window of the beautiful dining room into the park which spread itself over several acres of ground just across the street from his home.

"Harry, dear, why do you not eat?" remarked his wife. Harry Benton smiled, but as he did so a tear glistened on his cheek.

"For some reason," he answered, "I awoke an hour before day this morning and memory insisted on taking me on a journey over the past and carrying me on a ramble through the scenes of my childhood, and as I sit here the sight of those trees in the park remind me of old Ozark's grand forests. I like to think of those old scenes, and by the way, wife, come to think about it, it is three years this month since we were down home on a visit. It doesn't seem possible that it is so long. We get so absorbed with our business here in this big wicked city that the years flit by like dreams and we do not realize how long we have been away. I should like to take a stroll this morning along the old creek where we boys used to swim. I'd like to visit the old schoolhouse in the walnut grove where we used to spend so many idle hours. Three years ago when we were down there I visited that old schoolhouse. It looked just about like it did twenty-five or thirty years ago, when you and I were there. I sat on the old limestone rock beneath the old locust-tree where we used to play dare base. The old play ground is just the same. There was the ballground where we used to play 'town ball.' The same old stone was there that we used for second base."

As Harry Benton thus spoke his wife and children listened intently, and when the meal was finished and the Bible was brought for the morning worship, the whole family was in a serious frame of mind. Benton went on to say, "And when we talk of home scenes, I always think of father and his godly influence upon my life. As I look across the years, I see myself an ignorant awkward country boy; but there is one thing for which I shall always thank my God, and that is that I was blessed with a Christian father. Throughout the years his saintly life has been a benediction to me. The most sacred picture that hangs on the wall of my memory is that of my father with the big family Bible on his lap and all the children gathered around him and Mother for the worship of his God. Well do I remember when he used to pray for us, naming us out one by one and asking God to make us useful men and women. And oh, how he used to be persecuted by the Mount Olivet people. Well do I remember how one morning when Father was on his way to milk your father's cows he was met by Deacon Gramps, who beat him so shamefully. That night in family worship Father prayed so fervently and asked God to forgive Gramps and save him from his wicked ways. The impressions I received during those stirring days never will leave me. I tell you, Eva, it meant something for Father to stand true as he did, and I think heaven will be especially sweet to those who have suffered as he has suffered."

When he had left off speaking and the family knelt in prayer, Harry Benton's voice trembled with emotion as he prayed for all those back home whom he remembered, and especially for his father.

When the morning chores were done and Harry Benton started to the Full Salvation Mission, which mission he had superintended and supported for a number of years, he was met on his front porch by a Western Union messenger boy, who took from beneath his blue cap a slip of yellow paper and handed it to him. This is how it read: "Come, Father very low."

Benton telephoned one of his brethren to take charge of the Mission, and after earnestly beseeching the Lord to spare his father until his bedside could be reached, he and his wife made hasty arrangements to start, and were soon speeding across the fertile fields of Illinois. They crossed the mighty Mississippi, changed trains in St. Louis' big Union Depot, and after a few hours' ride their train was gliding past old familiar scenes of bygone days.

"Dobbinsville, Dobbinsville," shouted the porter as he thrust his face in at the door of the coach. Three short jerks at the signal cord--swish, swish, swish--back from the engine--t-oot-oot-oot--a sudden let-up in speed, a screech of the airbrakes, a bang of the door, and the Texas Canon-Ball made one of its seldom stops at Dobbinsville and Harry Benton and his family stepped to the platform.

A thirty-minute ride through the country in a neighbor's automobile and once more in life Harry Benton stepped foot upon the premises of his childhood. His prayer had been answered. His father seemed to be dying during the night, but with the coming of morning he revived and regained consciousness. When Harry and Eva entered the room where his father lay, the old saint seemed as happy as a child and much rejoiced at seeing Harry and Eva and their babies, who were the last of a great flock of sons and sons-in-law and daughters and daughters-in-law and grandchildren and great-grandchildren to arrive.

"Precious in the sight of the Lord is the death of his saints." Since Jake Benton's conversion, more than a quarter of a century previously to this time, his life had been one continuous sermon--a sermon more eloquent than any ever preached from a pulpit. But if the sermon of his life was eloquent, that of his death was more so. According to his simple philosophy, life was just a sort of lodging-place beside the long road to eternity, and death, to him, was not a leaving home, but rather a starting for home.

When he gathered his loved ones about his bedside on the day following the arrival of Harry and his family, to say goodbye, it was not the goodbye of one who was entering upon a dark and perilous journey to parts unknown, but that of one sustained by an unfailing faith that he was entering upon an abode in the eternal mansion, where he should wait but a brief period for the coming of those he loved.

Just as the purple shadows of the October evening were lengthening, the end was drawing near. The hoary patriarch called his children all by name--Harry and Eva, Joe and his wife, Albert and his wife, Nancy and her husband, Hannah and her husband, and Hattie, the unmarried daughter yet at home--and they all gathered in the room where death was to be a guest.

The grandchildren, happy and care-free, unconscious of what life is and of what death means, were called in from their places of play, and told that Grandpa was leaving them. The little tots, bless them, came in and stood around the old-fashioned bedstead all unmindful of the significance of a meeting of time and eternity. They gathered around and gazed into the old saint's face, where death and life alternately wrote their names. As they passed around one by one by the head of the bed, the old man laid his withered hands upon each little head and pronounced his blessing. Then he began to talk.

"If this is death," he said, "it is a blessed thing to die. The way has been long and the road rough, at times, but now it is all over. I have suffered a few things for Jesus' sake, but how unworthy I have been of all the love He has shown me. I have only one dying request to make of my loved ones, and it is the same as my living request has been, that you all live for God and meet me over there. Oh, I am so happy. How I love Jesus, and on His bosom I shall rest forever." His voice grew fainter. "Just one more step and I am there." The loved ones hovered nearer. A soft white hand was laid upon his brow. It was the hand of Hattie. Subdued sobs were heard about the room. "Don't weep, dear children," he faintly murmured: "I am just passing into--I see the darling's hands--no pale cheeks--how sweet--about my neck--this Rose--Rose's Savior Papa's Savior too. Let's go--." He was dead--and blessed are the dead which die in the Lord.